VARIETY TALES: KADEN'S DREAM

WORDS BY Jonathan Alexander

with Beth Snider & Tamara Dever

ILLUSTRATED BY Beth Snider

varietykc™
the children's charity

Inspired by Chief Inclusion Officer Deborah Wiebrecht
To learn more or make a donation, please visit our website at VarietyKC.org.

Cover & interior design by TLC Book Design, TLCBookDesign.com
Illustrated by Beth Snider

ISBN: 979-8-218-01075-1

This book is made possible by
the Meyer Family:
Chad, Lori, Andrew, Jack, and Brooks

On what should have been a normal Saturday,
Kaden woke up and knew exactly which shoes to wear.

He never left the house without choosing the coolest pair,
and it was a long, important process—usually.

"It must be because it's game day," Kaden thought.

Though they always went to the soccer stadium
on game day, and drove the same way
and used the same entrance,

KADEN FELT SOMETHING SPECIAL IN THE AIR TODAY.

The stadium concourse was taller than
ten Kadens standing on top of each other.

It smelled of hot popcorn and nacho cheese. Yum!

Posters of tough-looking players lined the walls.

They were some of Kaden's favorites,
like Addison, Morgan, and Matt.

"Soccer is for everyone!" they read.

Kaden agreed, but he couldn't help wondering why
there wasn't a poster up there for someone like him.

Kaden wasn't exactly like others his age.

He spoke by typing on a computer and was in a wheelchair, after all.

SOCCER IS FOR EVERYONE!

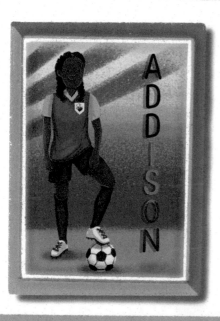

But that wasn't all Kaden was—
he was also just a kid like you.

A kid who picked out
the coolest shoes every morning,
who liked to go to soccer games
on the weekends;

A kid who was a grade ahead
in Math and Reading
and already had his cabinet picked out
for when he becomes the President.

People never just said "hi" to Kaden.

They always greeted his wheelchair first,
and him second.

Kaden was never just "Kaden."

Each weekend,
when Kaden went to the game,
he would cheer from the sidelines
as best he could.

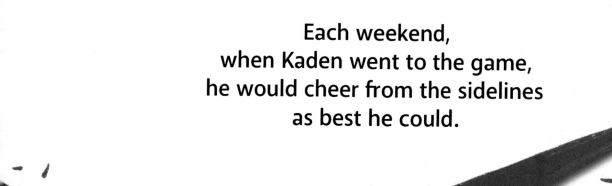

But he dreamed of
being on the field —
to just once, be the one
everyone else cheered for.

Lining the walls of the concourse were
posters of the local soccer stars.

Kaden had always dreamed of having
a poster of himself on the players' wall.

But there wasn't and he couldn't let that get him down.

If he did, who would cheer on his team?

The last poster wasn't of a player at all,
but of Variety's Mr. Heart himself.

He was a local legend who helped a variety of kids
to be active, be social, and belong.

Thinking about Mr. Heart
made Kaden feel a little better.

There were so many people bustling around that it
took a while for Kaden and his family to find their seats.

When people saw him, they often stopped in their tracks.

The stares didn't bother him, though; he was used to it.

He had to be positive today
because the team needed him to cheer.

Or so he thought.

Just as the players should have been warming up,
there was a tap on Kaden's shoulder.

It was Addison herself,
and she was smiling from ear to ear.

"WANT TO PLAY SOCCER WITH ME?"

Kaden had never been asked that before.

Today was special, after all!

"There isn't a field for someone like me,"
Kaden typed.

"You're right, there wasn't,
so, I called up a friend of mine to help."

A shadow passed over Kaden, and when he looked up,

He found himself staring at a smiling red face
he'd recognize anywhere.

"Addison told me you wanted to play soccer," Mr. Heart said.

"I couldn't believe there wasn't a sporting complex
for kids like you!

Don't you think we need to fix that?"
Kaden could only nod in response.

Mr. Heart smiled,
wider than
any smile Kaden
had ever seen.

"Well, thanks to
your dream,
we created
the nation's
most inclusive
sporting complex!

**NOW,
EVERYONE
CAN PLAY
TOGETHER.**

Let's go see it."

On their way out of the stadium, Addison said,

"WE HAVE A SURPRISE FOR YOU."

Kaden gasped as she showed him the new poster of him next to the other players.

"This shows everyone that you and other kids just like you can play Power Soccer with us!"

When they arrived at the new sporting complex,
Mr. Heart asked if Kaden wanted to play.

He didn't have to type a thing for them to know his answer.

Today, Kaden's team could do without his cheers.

TODAY, HE WOULD BE THE ONE GETTING CHEERED ON!

The field was bigger than Kaden thought possible.

It was long and green, and kids were already laughing as they kicked balls back and forth.

Best of all, they were kids like Kaden.

Mr. Heart and Addison led him
onto the field.

Kaden's wheelchair moved
smoothly over the new surface.

All the kids said "hi" to him,
not just to the wheelchair but to him.

The kid who picked out the
coolest shoes every morning,
and liked to go to soccer games
on the weekends,
and was a grade ahead in
Math and Reading,
and already had his cabinet picked out
for when he becomes the president.

Today, Kaden wasn't any of that, though.
He wasn't someone in a wheelchair,

Or a kid, or even "Kaden."

**FOR THE FIRST TIME,
HE WAS A SOCCER PLAYER.**

And so,
Kaden played
and played
and played,

and this time, everyone cheered for *him*.

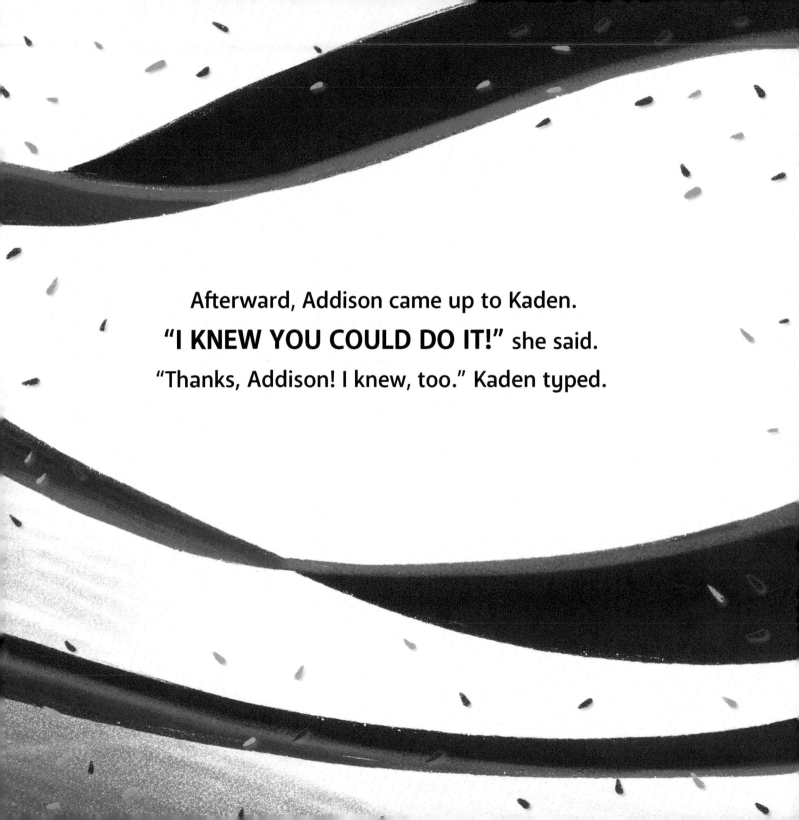

Afterward, Addison came up to Kaden.

"I KNEW YOU COULD DO IT!" she said.

"Thanks, Addison! I knew, too." Kaden typed.

Kaden began to play again.

He played until the sun started to set,
then decided that was enough for today.

He thanked Addison and Mr. Heart,
and told them he'd play soccer again tomorrow.

And the days after that.

HE WAS A SOCCER PLAYER, AFTER ALL.

But, of course, not without choosing
the coolest shoes for the day.

ABOUT KADEN

Kaden is a happy and passionate eight-year-old living with Spinal Muscular Atrophy type 1 (SMA). This means his muscles do not move his body independently. He uses a power wheelchair and uses a communication device as his voice. Kaden was diagnosed at six weeks old and we were told he had a 10% chance of seeing his second birthday. Doctors and SMA didn't know who they were messing with because he is determined to break all barriers set in front of him. His biggest goal in life is to be President to improve the lives of all future generations. Kaden might have SMA but he never lets it stop him from fighting for inclusion and equality, saying, "we are all human and deserve to be treated equally like humans. We are all pretty colors but together we make a beautiful rainbow."

ABOUT VARIETY

Variety Children's Charity of Greater Kansas City is a non-profit organization that raises funds for a variety of kids with special needs. Proceeds from *Variety Tales* will help fund equipment for kids with a Variety of disabilities and help remove barriers to help ALL Kids Be Active, Be Social and BELONG! To donate, visit VarietyKC.org.

FROM THE AUTHOR

"Growing up, I remember being hesitant to share my health issues with friends because I didn't want to be defined by the handful of multicolored pills I took each day. But I was extraordinarily lucky in having the support and care to assure me I wasn't just a list of limitations anymore, I was still just me. With this story, I want to let anyone walking a different path know the same thing I learned: that they're more than their differences. They can still dream and laugh and play—at the end of the day, they're still just a kid." – Jonathan Alexander

ABOUT THE ILLUSTRATOR

Beth Snider is located in the Kansas City area where she lives with her husband who is an elementary school teacher and a YouTuber with an outdoor adventure channel. They have three sons, a daughter, and a dog named Georgie. She enjoys creating delicious meals in the kitchen for her family. When she's not illustrating, you can find her cozying up on the couch, braiding her daughter's hair, a cup of coffee nearby, watching an episode of "Little House on the Prairie."